Wheeler's Good Time

Wheeler's

Good Time

by Daniel Schantz

Art by Ned O.

STANDARD PUBLISHING
Cincinnati, Ohio   2929

Library of Congress Cataloging in Publication Data

Schantz, Daniel.
   Wheeler's good time.

   Summary: Sonny and Earnest's attempt
to spend the summer doing good deeds
backfires in many comical and unexpected
ways.
   [1. Brothers—Fiction. 2. Conduct of
life—Fiction. 3. Humorous stories] I. Os-
tendorf, Ned, ill. II. Title.
PZ7.S3338Wi 1987   [Fic]   87-9909
ISBN 0-87403-320-9 (pbk.)

to Ralph and Joyce Haller
and their children, Lara,
Patti, and Michael

Contents

Bad Jokes 9
The Grass Prix 17
Cherry Pits 26
Grime Fighters 33
Housebroken 42
Pie Wars 51
The Diamond 60
Pulling Teeth 70
The Big Prize 78
Five Special Words 90

1 • Bad Jokes

Sonny and Earnest peeked in the garage door, trying not to explode with laughter.

"What's he doin'?" Earnest whispered. His dark eyes danced.

Sonny ducked his father's glance and rested his blond head against the side of the garage. He looked at the big red firecracker in his slender hand and grinned.

"Nothin'," he said. "He's just getting ready to change a tire."

"Okay, let's do it," Earnest urged.

Sonny pulled a matchbook from his pocket, pinched a match from it and held it nervously to the firecracker's fuse. The fuse sputtered and spit. With one smooth motion, Sonny lobbed the firecracker into the garage. It bounced to rest only inches from his father's feet.

For a few seconds Mr. Wheeler just stared at the smoking fuse. It crackled and sparkled, then slowly died out. The firecracker was not going to explode. But Mr. Wheeler did.

He grabbed the little bomb in his heavy hand and stomped outside. There he found the boys, clutching their stomachs with laughter.

He glared at Sonny and Earnest with a crimson face. His eyes blazed with anger. His hands were curled into great fists.

"If you two think this is funny," he roared, "then you have a very sick sense of humor!"

The smiles vanished from the boy's faces, and their eyes widened with fear. Neither of them moved an inch.

"But it's just a gag, Dad," Sonny muttered. "Here, see?" He turned the firecracker on end so his father could see it was only an empty cardboard tube with a fuse stuck in one end.

But Mr. Wheeler's face was purple. He

wrenched the tube from Sonny's hand and heaved it across the driveway and into the ditch. Then he grabbed Sonny by his left arm and pulled him up close to his face.

Sonny could smell his father's breath and could see the pupils of his eyes swelling and shrinking.

"Sonny, you are twelve years old, and you should be bright enough to know you don't throw *anything* with sparks anywhere near this garage." He waved his other arm about wildly as he spoke. "I've got gasoline, kerosene, propane, parts cleaner—a lot of stuff that could blow us all right off the block."

Sonny's body dangled limply from his father's massive hand. His face was as pale as his blond hair, and he was barely breathing.

Mr. Wheeler glared at Earnest. "Earnest! Did you put Sonny up to this?"

Earnest shook his head and played with his fingers. His mouth was puckered with fear and his short, stocky body seemed shorter than ever.

Mr. Wheeler let go of Sonny. He pointed to the house.

"You boys get to your rooms, and I don't want to see your faces till supper. Do you understand me?"

Sonny and Earnest nodded and aimed themselves obediently toward the big blue house.

"I am sick and tired of your jokes!" their father shouted after them. "And I'm going to put a stop to this nonsense once and for all!" He stood by the garage looking like a crazed gorilla. His mustache was twisted into a snarl and his face was as hard as cement.

Sonny and Earnest marched into the house and didn't stop moving until they got to the doorway of Sonny's bedroom.

"What did we do wrong?" Sonny whispered.

"I don't know," Earnest replied. "I've never seen Dad like this before. He *never* gets mad."

"I know. He looked like Rambo. I thought he was going to kill us. And I always thought he was a marshmallow."

"A cast iron marshmallow, if you ask me. Wonder what he's going to do to us?"

The two of them shut themselves up in their rooms. Earnest tried to read a book, and Sonny killed time bouncing a Nerf ball off the wall.

At supper time, Sonny and Earnest tiptoed to the kitchen and quietly sat down at the table. They kept glancing at their father's face to check his mood. He did not return their glances, but just stared at his plate and shoveled potatoes, beef, and noodles into his mouth. Sonny and Earnest said nothing as they did the same. Mrs. Wheeler kept up a steady chatter of news and gossip until she realized she was the only one talking. By then the meal was over.

Mr. Wheeler gave a certain look to his wife, and she quietly put away the milk and butter and left the room without looking back.

Sonny and Earnest peeked at each other, waiting for their father to say something.

At last he was finished. He wadded up his napkin and tucked it under the edge of his plate. The boys could see the good meal had lightened his mood a little, but still they said nothing for fear.

"Sonny . . . Earnest," their father began at last. "I am very unhappy with you two."

The boys blinked.

Mr. Wheeler cleared his throat. "I know you like to have fun, and I don't begrudge that for a moment. But these jokes have got to stop."

"We didn't mean any harm," Sonny blurted out.

"Maybe not, Sonny, but it's getting out of hand. I didn't mind too much when you filled my office with wadded up newspaper, even though it cost me an hour's work time to clean it all up."

Earnest pointed at Sonny. "That was *his* idea."

"I'm not interested in your excuses. Then when you hid my appointment book, you caused me a *lot* of trouble. Took me three days to calm down my customers."

The boys hung their heads.

"Which one of you loosened the lid of the salt shaker?"

Earnest meekly held up his hand.

"Well, your mother ruined an expensive casserole thanks to that little stunt. You can thank me for covering for you, or you'd be a tossed salad by now."

Sonny and Earnest grinned ever so slightly.

"Which one of you put clear plastic wrap over the toilet bowl?"

Again Earnest held up his hand.

"Earnest? What are you, the brains behind this crime organization?" Now he was grinning, and the boys began to relax a little.

Mr. Wheeler shook his head. "I'll never understand why they call them practical jokes. Nothing practical about them. How come you guys never pull any nice tricks, huh?" He began to gather up the plates and stack them in the sink. "Let's do these dishes before these noodles turn to glue."

Sonny washed, Earnest dried, and their father put the dishes in the cupboard.

"Why is it so easy for you boys to get into trouble and so hard for you to do good?"

Sonny shrugged. "I don't know . . . except, well, it's not *cool* to be good all the time."

"All the time? I'll settle for now and then!"

Sonny went on. "But Dad, if we went around being goody-goody, our friends would laugh us right out of town."

Mr. Wheeler's brow showed deep lines. "Then you mean you're *afraid* to be good, is that it?"

"Well, no," Earnest piped up. "I mean, I'm not afraid to *do* good things, I just don't want to be *seen*, or somebody will think I'm showing off. Or they'll think I'm just being plain weird."

"That's true about being weird," Sonny said. "I'm afraid somebody will think I'm trying to brown nose someone if I do good things. Besides, the good stuff is no challenge. It's too easy."

Mr. Wheeler gave the boys one last serious look. "Maybe not as easy as you think, Sonny. Look, sneak and do good if you have to, but I'll tell you this—there is no limit to how much good you can do in this world if you can get over those silly fears. And one more thing." He pointed his thick, strong finger at the boys and frowned. "If I see any more of these practical jokes, you will spend the rest of the summer in your rooms."

The boys nodded.

"Then you aren't going to punish us?" Earnest asked.

Mr. Wheeler picked up a big spoon and rapped it on the kitchen counter three times like a gavel.

"I, Judge Wheeler, hereby sentence Sonny and Earnest to do good deeds. This court is adjourned."

2 • The Grass Prix

The little town of Mulberry was just waking up. Sonny and Earnest lay on their backs on the hood of Sonny's old Studebaker. The August morning sun was already warm, but a cool northerly breeze felt good on their skin.

"I really feel rotten," Earnest said, removing his sunglasses.

"I wondered what that smell was," Sonny replied.

"No, I mean it, Sonny. I feel really bad that we got Dad all upset. I've never seen him like that before. Not ever. I think I hate myself."

"Yeah, I know what you mean. I guess we fumbled that one. Dad is the greatest. He shoulda hung us up by our thumbs."

Earnest sat up. "Maybe we ought to do something *good* for a change."

Sonny opened one eye. "*Bor*-ing," he growled.

Earnest nodded. "But no more boring than sitting around here. I'll betcha I could do more good stuff than you could."

Sonny opened his other eye. "Oh? You must have a lot of friends."

"Sonny," Earnest snapped, "I could do more good stuff in one week than you've done in your whole life."

Sonny sat up. He stuck out his hand. "Is that a challenge?"

Earnest clutched Sonny's hand. "It's a *deal*." Then a puzzled look came to his face. "But what are we gonna do? This is all new to me."

Sonny shrugged. "I don't know, let's ask Mom. She always has good ideas."

The two of them leaped off the car hood and raced to the garage office.

Earnest explained the challenge to his mother. "So, we need some good stuff to do," he added.

Mrs. Wheeler leaned back in her chair. "Well, give me a minute to get over the shock," she replied. "It isn't every day you want to do something good." She stared out the window, thinking. "There is one thing I can think of. You know the Paynes? They've been on vacation for two weeks. I was by there yesterday, and their lawn is a jungle."

Sonny looked at Earnest and grinned. The boys whirled around and headed for the storage shed at full speed.

Earnest got there first and grabbed the new lawnmower, a bright yellow machine with ball-bearing wheels. Sonny crashed into the shed, then jumped up and grabbed the handle of the old mower, a dull red machine with a black engine.

"Got it!" he yelled.

"Got what?" Earnest asked.

"The old mower. It's easier to push than the new one. It's lighter."

"Yeah, sure, you're just trying to get me to give you the new one." Earnest picked up the gas can, but it rose in his hand like a balloon. "Uh-oh, we need fuel."

The boys headed for the gas station, taking turns carrying the can. As they passed by Cherry's house, Sonny stopped and stared.

"What's wrong?"

"I don't know," Sonny explained. "But look. The shades are drawn, and look at her flower bed."

"Yeah, she never lets it get weedy like that. And the watering puddle is all dried up."

"Maybe we oughta check it out," Sonny said, stepping up on the porch. He knocked on the door and waited a long time. Finally the door opened a little, and Cherry peeked through the crack.

Sonny peered back at her. "Hey, Cherry, what's up? You okay?"

Cherry looked tired. Her skin was pale, and her freckles had faded from being indoors. Her red hair looked like it hadn't been washed in a month. In a low, whispery voice she said, "My grandma has ammonia."

"Huh?" Sonny asked.

"She's sick. I can't talk to you. I'll see ya." Slowly she shut the door and locked it.

Sonny rejoined Earnest. "She says her grandma has ammonia."

"She means pneumonia," Earnest said. "That's kinda serious, isn't it?"

"Yeah. Must be pretty bad for Cherry to let her garden go like that."

"Hey," Earnest added, "as soon as we get this lawn mowed we can make her our next project."

"Okay, first one to put a smile on her face wins a round."

At last the boys had the mowers filled and ready to go. Sure enough, when they got there the lawn was a foot high, and the grass was beginning to form seed.

"I'll take this half," Sonny said, pointing.

"I might know you would pick the easy side," Earnest whined.

"But your mower has more power than mine. You can cut that heavy stuff better."

"Excuses, excuses."

Earnest looked over his half of the lawn, picking up dead branches and tin cans and other trash. He stepped off the distance and made some calculations in his mind.

"Will you come on, for crying out loud," Sonny complained. "This is a race, not a garden show."

Finally Earnest was ready.

Sonny grabbed a short stick and held it to his mouth like a microphone.

"Ladies and gentlemen, welcome to the annual Grass Prix. In the yellow mower, Earnest Wheeler. This mower has never been in a race before. Will

it perform? That's the question in everyone's mind. And in the red mower with the hot black engine, Son-ny Wheel-er, the favorite in this race. This red mower has seen a lot of checkered flags, folks. Gentlemen, start your engines."

Earnest's mower started with one tug of the rope. Sonny's mower belched thick smoke as it sputtered to life on the seventh pull of the rope. Sonny pulled out his handkerchief and waved it to the ground to start the race.

Earnest pulled out ahead, while Sonny adjusted his mower further. But with his long legs, Sonny soon caught up with Earnest. Now the two of them were criss-crossing the lawn at breakneck speed. Earnest's short legs blurred like a gopher crossing a busy highway. Sonny bounded along like an ostrich trying to take off and fly.

Soon Earnest began to tire. He stopped to remove his good shirt, and he hung it carefully on a nearby lilac bush.

Sonny pulled out ahead, but his mower was missing sections of grass as it belched huge clouds of oily blue smoke. At each corner he spun around like a ballet dancer, so as not to lose a second. He was near the house when *wham!* the mower stopped cold.

"We've got a pileup at the corner," Sonny shrieked. "The driver of the red mower has hit a rock." He shoved the mower forward and restarted it, but Earnest passed him by with a smug smile on his face.

Earnest bobbed and bounced along proudly, glancing now and then to see if Sonny was gaining on him. And he was. Earnest took a deep breath and lunged forward even faster, but halfway down his row he abruptly stopped and stared at the grass in front of him. Then he stooped down and pulled apart a clump of tall grass. There he saw a nest of baby rabbits. He blinked at the pink-white babies, and they blinked back, their little bodies trembling with fear. Earnest smiled at the baby bunnies, then glanced at his brother who was flying across the yard behind his mower. Quickly Earnest zigged his mower around the bunnies and kept moving.

The yard was almost done now. It looked clean and neat and smelled sweet like new hay. Earnest licked salty sweat from his upper lip and headed down the last row with all the strength he could find. Behind him he could feel the vibration of Sonny's mower coming up fast. Now the two of them were side by side with ten feet to go. Earnest pounded the ground with his feet, his face grimly set on winning this race.

All of a sudden Sonny gave his mower a big shove and let go of the handle. Like a guided missile it shot to the end of the row and into the vegetable garden, where it bumped to a halt against a big squash. Sonny had won.

Both boys collapsed on the lawn, panting for air. Then slowly, silently, they staggered over to the outside faucet and unhooked the hose. Sonny lay on his back under the faucet and let a stream of the cold liquid splash into his mouth and all over his hot face. At last he turned the faucet over to Earnest.

"Well, Earnest," he panted, "one for me . . . and . . . none for you."

Earnest spit a long stream of water at Sonny, and Sonny dashed away only to collapse again on the lawn.

3 • Cherry Pits

After lunch, Sonny leaped up from the table, grabbed his pocket knife from the utility drawer and dashed outside.

"Where's he going in such a rush?" Mrs. Wheeler asked Earnest. She wiped the counter dry and wrung out the cloth in the sink.

Earnest washed the last of his sandwich down with lemonade. "Oh, he's gonna try to cheer up Cherry with some wildflowers."

"Oh? Is Cherry feeling low?"

"She's in the pits, believe me. She says her

grandma has ammonia. She means pneumonia, doesn't she?"

"Yes. That not good news at all. People die from that, especially the aged."

"Oh, really? No wonder she's acting so funny. You know, if anything happens to her grandma, she's out on the street. Her parents are separated, and they don't show much interest in her."

"Yes, I do know. That poor little girl." Mrs. Wheeler stared out the kitchen window, thinking.

"Mom, what can I do to cheer her up? I mean, what do girls like?"

"Well, I'm sure Sonny is on the right track with flowers."

"Sure, but she's already got millions of flowers. She grows 'em."

Mrs. Wheeler nodded. "Yes, you may be right about that. I do know she likes chocolate, especially truffles."

"Truffles?"

"Uh-huh. But they are expensive, I warn you. The drugstore sells them."

"What else?"

Mrs. Wheeler dried her hands. "I don't really know, Earnest. Anyhow, cheering people up can be mighty tricky business. Sometimes nothing works. Sometimes only God can cheer a person."

Earnest looked deep in thought. Finally he got up and went to his room where he wiggled some money out of his safe-bank. He put on clean dress clothes and headed for the drugstore.

Meanwhile Sonny was tromping through the meadow beside Long Branch Lake. In each hand he carried a bucket, and the big pocket knife bulged in his pants pocket. He swished and leaped through the meadow grasses, stopping to clip clumps of pink sweet peas for one bucket and blue morning glories for the other bucket. He added handsful of meadow vetch for green. When his buckets were overflowing, he started back up the hill. Halfway up he stopped and stared at a patch of big wild sunflowers. His eyes gleamed as he fished the knife from his pocket. Up close the sunflowers were even bigger than he first thought. Each bold yellow flower was a foot wide and the centers were densely packed with seeds.

Sonny gripped a sunflower stem about halfway down. It was as thick as his own arm. With great effort he sawed through the rugged stem and lowered the flower to the ground.

"Oof! These suckers are heavy. Oughta call 'em tonflowers. This ought to bring a smile or three."

He cut two more of the massive blooms and rested all three of them on his shoulders like baseball bats. He carried both buckets with one hand.

At home, Sonny stuffed the big sunflowers into an old metal milk bucket that was almost as big as him. Then he packed the three buckets into his wagon and set off for Cherry's house.

When he arrived, he noticed the shades were still drawn. He rested a few minutes, studying Cherry's flower garden. Then he began to tug at the weeds in the garden, pitching them on to the lawn behind him. He hooked up the hose and drenched the wilted flowers. When he was satisfied, he wheeled the buckets of flowers up to the porch and set them by the front door. Then he leaned on the bell with his thumb.

The door slowly opened. "Yes?" Cherry said, coldly.

Sonny put on his widest smile. "Hi, there, gorgeous! Some lovely flowers for the lovely lady. Enjoy!"

Cherry did not return the smile, and she was not looking at his flowers. Rather she was staring at her flower garden. A cloud spread over her face. "What have you done to my garden?" she asked in a tight, clipped voice.

"Just a little extra touch," Sonny sang out. "Got rid of a few weeds and put a little fresh dew on the patch." He looked pleased with himself.

Cherry frowned. In a quivering voice she said, "Those are not weeds. Those are my amaranthus. They may look like weeds, but they aren't." Her tiny forehead was pinched with irritation, and her red hair seemed to flicker like flames.

"Oh," was all Sonny could think to say, and right away he knew even that was too much.

Cherry squeezed the edge of the door and prepared to slam it. "And you never ever water flowers in the hot sun. It burns them." Her voice warbled with anger and tears. She shut the door firmly.

Sonny just stood there feeling stupid. His face was hot and his lower lip was drooping.

Slowly he dragged the buckets of flowers back to the wagon. He started home, then stopped at the flower garden. With a sad look he picked up the flowers he thought were weeds and tried to replant them, but they were limp and lifeless. He shuffled on down the street with the wagon trailing behind him. When he came to a vacant lot, he dumped the flowers into a tall stand of weeds.

Meanwhile Earnest headed for Cherry's house

with a small white sack of chocolate truffles and a get-well card for Cherry's grandmother.

As he ambled up the sidewalk, he noticed the garden had been weeded, and he smelled the fragrance of sun-warmed water on flowers.

"Hmmmmm," he said to himself. "Cherry must be doing better. She weeded the garden."

He stood at the door, tucking in his shirt. Then he peeked in the sack to see if the truffles were okay, and finally he rang the bell.

He hummed to himself as he waited. A long time passed and no one answered the door.

He rang again. Still no one answered.

Dong, dong, he rang again. Still nothing happened. He rapped on the door with his fist, then peeked in the living room window.

"I know she's here," he comforted himself. "She wouldn't leave her grandma."

Once more he hammered on the door, but no one responded.

At last he slipped the card into the door edge and sat the little white sack on the porch floor where she would be sure to see it. With that he turned and headed for home at a gallop.

The hot afternoon sun bore down on the little sack of chocolates.

4 • Grime Fighters

Earnest folded up the newspaper and dropped it into the wastebasket. With a handful of clippings, he strolled into Sonny's room.

Sonny looked up from the car magazine he was reading. "Whatcha got, Earnest?"

Earnest thumbed through the clippings. "Some ideas for our next project. Here's a story about teenagers who have been trashing the city parking lot. And some people are complaining about all the graffiti on the post office walls."

"So what are we supposed to do about that?

We didn't do it. It's not our problem."

Earnest stared blankly at his brother. "I thought we were looking for good things to do. We can pick up the trash and erase the graffiti."

Sonny winced. "Oh. I was afraid that's what you meant. Don't you have anything easier?"

Well, they need someone to tutor second graders in reading, and a lady needs an air conditioner moved . . . and they need volunteers to collect money."

"Forget that stuff. Let's go with the trash pickup."

Sonny and Earnest arrived at the city parking lot before any shoppers or city employees had arrived.

"Here, you'd better wear these gloves," Earnest said.

Sonny looked at the white garden gloves scornfully. "Get those outta my face. I'm not wearing any sissy gloves."

Next Earnest handed Sonny a plastic trash bag and opened one for himself. Sonny just kept prancing around, glancing to the left and right. "C'mon, let's get this over with before somebody sees us." He looked at his watch. "This lot will start filling up in a half hour."

Earnest picked up a soft pebble and scribbled some numbers on the pavement. "Okay, here's the rules. Bottle caps and pop tabs are worth ten points cause they're small. Can cartons and paper are worth five points. Bottles are two points, and everything else is worth one point."

"Yeah, yeah," Sonny growled. "Let's get on with it." He tugged at his pants and swiveled his head, looking for people who might be watching.

"As soon as the first car arrives, it's over," Earnest explained. "All right, on your mark, get set . . . and, *go!*"

Sonny shook open his sack and began stuffing it with everything in sight. He ran, slid, crawled, and reached for trash as fast as he could move. In no time his sack was heavy and he had to use both hands to drag it around.

Meanwhile, Earnest ignored heavy bottles, picking up bottlecaps and pop tabs and paper. His sack was light and easy to handle.

A car drove slowly by. Instantly Sonny turned his head so the driver would not recognize him. When it passed, he returned to his wild scramble for trash.

The lot was almost entirely clean when a city car pulled into the lot and parked by city hall.

"That's it!" Earnest hollered, and the two boys started dragging their collections over to the alley, where a giant trash pickup sat looking like a monster with an open mouth.

Suddenly a city trash truck rumbled into the lot. The workers hopped off the back. One of them glared at Sonny and Earnest.

"Hey! What are you kids up to? Are you trying to put us out of work? Get outta here!"

The boys sat down in the alley to examine their work. Sonny's sack was bulging at the seams and torn in two places. Earnest's sack was half full.

"I found a quarter and a dime," Earnest boasted. "But let's count this trash for points."

Sonny compared his sack with Earnest's. "Hey, I got twice as much as you. I'll win easy."

But when the points were added up, Earnest had won by fifty points.

"You always cheat," Sonny complained. "You and your complicated rules nobody else can understand."

"Well, the score is tied now," Earnest said. "You won the lawnmower race and I won this one."

Sonny sneered. "This just proves what a trashy guy you are."

Next the boys headed for the post office. Although it wouldn't open for another hour, the entry way was always open. That's where all the graffiti covered the walls.

Sonny was reading some of the fine print when Earnest handed him an eraser, a damp sponge, and a pad of steel wool. "Have you read this stuff?" Sonny asked. "It's putrid. Where do guys think up all these strange things?"

"Well," Earnest grumbled, "Are you going to read it or erase it? I'll take this wall, and you take that one. First one done is the winner."

"What? No tricky rules? Wait a minute ..." Sonny looked closely at his wall, then compared it to Earnest's all. "No! *You* take this wall and I'll take *that* one. You picked the easy wall."

Earnest threw up his hands and rolled his eyes. "Whatever his majesty desires. Let's just get started. Ready? Okay ... *go!*"

Sonny started at the left end, furiously erasing everything in sight. He left the sponge and pad lying on the floor.

Earnest took his damp sponge and went over the whole wall first. Many of the scribbles washed away easily. Next he erased pencil marks; then he tackled the tough stains with the steel wool pad. In no time he was far ahead of Sonny.

The boys were almost through when a police cruiser stopped outside, and a patrolman got out. He adjusted his gun belt and wrenched open the post office door. Earnest was ahead of Sonny and only seconds away from finishing. Neither of them noticed the police car.

"Hey!" the patrolman called out. Sonny and Earnest looked around and saw the officer beckoning to them to come to him.

"Yes, *you*," the man called. Sonny and Earnest stared blankly at each other, then shuffled over to the man.

"You boys come with me, please." He turned and strode outside and opened the door of the cruiser, motioning for the boys to get inside.

The boys squeezed into the back seat and sat down. They noticed the car was filled with a smoky, electrical smell, and Sonny couldn't take his eyes off the heavy-duty shotgun strapped between the seats.

The patrolman held his radio mike to his lips. "Car seven here. I'm checking out some juvenile vandalism at the post office."

Sonny and Earnest stared at each other with big eyes.

"May I have you boys' names, please?"

"I'm Sonny. Sonny Wheeler. This is my brother, Earnest."

The patrolman scribbled the names on a note pad. "Boys," he said at last, "I don't think I need to tell you that's government property you were defacing in there. Suppose you tell me why?"

"Defacing!" Earnest blurted out. "We weren't defacing, we were erasing it." He held up his eraser.

"Is that true?" he asked, looking at Sonny.

"Yes, Sir, honest, Sir. I can show you, Sir."

The three traipsed back into the post office.

"See," Sonny said. "The walls are clean."

The patrolman studied the wall closely, tracing his fingers over the remaining smudges. Then a smile came to his face. "Well," he said in a pleased voice, "it looks like I have falsely accused you boys." He squeezed the boys' shoulders affectionately. "I don't know what got into you boys, but I wish we had a few more like you."

When the patrolman had left, the boys leaned against the counter and sighed long sighs of relief.

"I don't know about this good deed stuff," Sonny said. "Maybe it's not such a hot idea after all." He wiped a bead of sweat from his forehead.

On the way home the two of them passed by Cherry's house. Earnest noticed the blinds were still drawn. In the door edge was his get-well card, and the sack of truffles was melted in a blob. Earnest winced, thinking of how much he had spent on the chocolates.

5 • Housebroken

Early morning at the Wheeler house was an orchestra of sounds: the buzz of an electric razor, the hum of blow dryers, the "boom, boom, boom" of Sonny's stereo, the TV weather report, and pots and pans banging in the kitchen. To these sounds was added the ring of the phone.

"Hello," Mrs. Wheeler answered. "Uh-huh. Oh, I see. Yes, of course. Oh, my. Oh, my, I'm so sorry. All right, I will. Yes, thank you. Bye-bye."

"Who was that?" Earnest asked as he took a seat at the kitchen table.

"That was Mrs. Payne. She thanks you two for mowing her lawn . . ."

Sonny and Earnest smiled a smug smile.

". . . but one of you ran over the garden hose nozzle and shattered it to pieces. She would like a new one."

Earnest scowled at Sonny. "You told me you hit a *rock*."

Sonny scowled back. "How should I know what it was? I was in a hurry, remember? Don't get hyper, I'll buy the lady a new nozzle." Then under his breath he muttered, "This good deed stuff is getting to be a pain in the pocket. Chee, you would think people would be grateful."

"Mom," Earnest said, "What are we gonna do about Cherry? She's still not talking to anyone."

Mrs. Wheeler just shook her head. "I dunno, boys, I dunno."

"You could serenade her," Mr. Wheeler said, reaching for some toast. "We used to do that in my time."

"What's serenade?"

"Oh, you know, sing to her at her window."

Sonny looked at Earnest with a smirk on his face, as if to say, "You gotta be kidding."

"Singing is *out*, Dad," Earnest said firmly. Then

he got a gleam in his eye. "But maybe we could put on a little act or something. You know, like the Three Stooges, or hey! She *loves* Laurel and Hardy."

Mrs. Wheeler began gathering up the dishes. "Not to rush anyone, but I've got a big day. The ladies from church are coming over tonight, and I've got to clean this house from top to bottom. And before I can do that I've got a week's work in the office."

Earnest and Sonny paid no attention. "We could do the one where Laurel and Hardy are trying to move a piano up the stairs," Earnest went on, brainstorming to himself.

"Naw," Sonny objected, "that's too hard. How we gonna get a piano to Cherry's house?"

"Yeah, I suppose you're right. But we could handle the one where they are playing their horns on the street for money and they get into a big fight, remember?"

Sonny's eyes lit up. "All right! And we could add a big pie fight!"

Mr. and Mrs. Wheeler went to the garage to work, leaving the boys at the table to talk over their plans.

Then Earnest jumped up from the table. "Hey,

let's surprise Mom and clean the house for her."

A look of horror came over Sonny. "What?! Another cleaning job? I'm tired of messin' with trash."

"Aw, quit your griping. This won't take long. Do you want to win or not?"

"What's the score, anyway?"

"Two for me," Earnest said, "And one for you. I was winning the graffiti wipe when the law stopped us."

"What do we get if we make Cherry smile?"

"First one to do that," Earnest said, "gets two extra points."

Sonny nodded.

Earnest grabbed a notepad and looked over the house. He made a list of things to be done—vacuuming, dusting, cleaning the bathrooms, washing and waxing the kitchen floor, emptying the wastebaskets.

"Do you want the upstairs or the downstairs, Sonny? I don't want to hear you accusing me of cheating."

"Let's flip for it," Sonny suggested. He spun a quarter from his thumb. "Heads, I get upstairs." The coin landed tails.

The boys gathered the equipment they would need, and Sonny dived into the downstairs job, starting with wastebaskets.

Upstairs, Earnest swept floors, cleaned the bath, then snapped the dusting brush onto the vacuum cleaner wand. He opened a window for fresh air and kicked the switch to "on." Earnest attacked the furniture eagerly, ending up with his mother's dresser. He was singing to himself and swishing the wand back and forth happily when a rattling noise stopped him cold.

"Uh-oh!" he said aloud. "I just sucked up Mom's jewelry." He shut off the machine and rattled the hose. "Awww, great, just great. It's all the way inside the machine." He sat down on the floor, opened the vacuum cleaner and pulled out the paper bag. He squeezed the fat bag over and over, trying to feel the jewelry, but he wasn't sure. With a fingernail file he slit open the bag and laid it on the floor. His fingers carefully sorted through the tangle of dust and hair, until he found three earrings and a diamond ring. Just as he held them up to the light, a strong breeze ruffled the bedroom curtains, and the pile of dust began flying around the room like a nest of angry bees.

Earnest choked on the dust. He slammed the

window down, then fled downstairs to the pantry for a new dust bag, but when he peered in the box, it was empty.

"What's up?" Sonny asked, peeking around the corner.

"You don't want to know," Earnest yelled. "Be right back." He disappeared out the kitchen door, headed for the hardware store.

Meanwhile, Sonny had finished all his work except for the kitchen. Carefully he cleaned the stove and refrigerator, then poured a fresh bucket of water to do the floor.

"What does she use for cleaning floors?" he wondered out loud. He peered under the sink. Finding nothing, he went to the bathroom and searched its cabinets. He grew impatient.

"This will have to do," he said to himself. He snatched a bottle off the edge of the bathtub and squirted big globs into his bucket.

Sonny was just starting to scrub the kitchen floor when Earnest crashed through the door and raced upstairs with a sack in his hand.

Sonny stacked the kitchen chairs on top of the table and knelt to scrub the floor. At first the soapy water worked fine, and he hummed to himself as he scrubbed. But the more he worked the sponge, the more suds seemed to build up on the floor. By the time he reached the middle of the room, the suds were heaping up like little snowy mountains, and great blobs of bubbles clung to his face and arms.

"What is this stuff, anyway?" He reached for the bottle and squinted at the label. "Castile Shampoo. The sudsiest shampoo money can buy."

Quickly he dumped the bucket in the sink and filled it with clear rinse water. But the more water he applied to the floor, the more suds billowed up.

Ten buckets of water later, he had the foam under control. Then he opened the windows and set up a fan to hasten the drying.

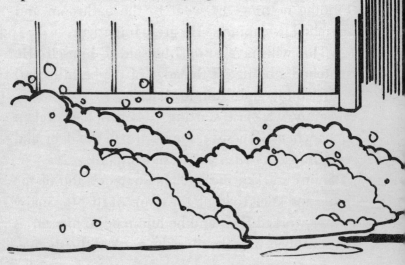

While the floor dried, Sonny tiptoed upstairs to see how Earnest was doing. When he saw Earnest sitting in a pile of dirt, he snickered to himself. Then he scampered back down to search for floor wax.

From the dark pantry he grasped a large spray can that said, "Wax." And in fine print, "Lemon Fresh."

"Sounds good," he said. "I just spray it on and wipe it off."

When the floor was dry, Sonny started in the corner of the room: spray-wipe, spray-wipe, spray-wipe. He scooted backwards like a crawdad as he worked. Before long he was done. He stood up to admire his work, sniffing the pleasant aroma of lemon from the spray. He was careful not to step on the gleaming floor.

Quickly he put away his cleaning tools and sprang up the steps to announce his victory.

"Two and two!" Sonny shouted when he reached the top landing. "We're even up."

Earnest shut off the vacuum cleaner and sighed. "Right now I don't care who wins," he said. "I'm just glad I got this mess cleaned up." Bits of dust and hair clung to his clothes and face.

Sonny plopped down on the bed to rest. "That's *it* for me," he groaned. "No more cleaning jobs. My back is broken, and my hands are water-logged. How does Mom do it? She must be made out of steel cables or somethin'."

"Hey," Earnest said, "aren't you the one who said doing good is too easy?"

6 • Pie Wars

Sonny and Earnest watched out the window, waiting for their mother to return to the kitchen. It was eleven-thirty before she left the office and walked briskly toward the house. The boys waited in the doorway between the kitchen and the dining room. They could hardly breathe from excitement.

The kitchen door opened and their mother appeared. She stopped just inside the door and looked around. She sniffed the air.

"Surprise!" the boys squealed from the doorway. "We cleaned the whole house for you!"

Their mother looked at the kitchen sink and the floors. "You . . . you did what? Whoooooooops!" She slipped on the shiny floor and fell, catching herself with her hands. "What the . . ." She tried to get up, but back down she went. There she sat, rubbing the polished floor and smelling her palm. She was not hurt, but she was plainly embarrassed.

"Boys, can I ask you what you used to wax this floor?" Her face was pink, and her blue eyes searched the boys' faces.

Sonny held up the can of wax. "This stuff, see? It says *wax*, right here. And it even smells good, huh?"

Mrs. Wheeler rolled her eyes and groaned. "Sonny, that is *furniture* wax, not *floor* wax. I thought I recognized that smell. Sonny, that product is so slippery I have to be careful even with furniture. One overspray and someone could break a leg."

Sonny hung his head, his lower lip protruding. "I—I didn't know there's a difference."

Mrs. Wheeler struggled to her feet and brushed her fading blond hair from her eyes. She was not smiling, but neither was she frowning.

"Even so, Sonny, this is the nicest thing anyone has done for me in a long time, and I appreciate your efforts." She reached for her purse and handed Sonny a five-dollar bill. "You'd better go get us some burgers. I can't cook in here till I rub this down with ammonia." She tested the floor with her toes. "I just hope I can get it off before the meeting tonight."

Sonny and Earnest took the afternoon off, too tired even to think about good deeds. They lay around in their rooms, reading and tinkering until supper.

After supper the two of them trudged up to the attic and came back with two large boxes of old clothes, which they took to Sonny's room. For a few minutes they rummaged through the boxes, tossing things all over the beds.

"Phew, these things stink," Sonny said. He pulled out a big pair of brown pants and tugged them on over his jeans. They were several sizes too big. "Hey, these are perfect! I'll be Laurel. You can be Hardy."

Earnest pulled on some dark pants and a white shirt. "The collar goes up, like this," he explained to Sonny. "You wear the bow tie, and I'll wear this long tie."

Sonny buttoned his shirt and put on a red bow tie, then slipped into an old brown suit coat. "How do I look, Earnest?"

"Not bad for a creep. Anything can improve your looks. Here, you need to comb your hair up into a porcupine." He found a jar of first-aid jelly and smeared it into Sonny's hair, then teased it straight up.

Sonny stood in front of the mirror and grinned at himself, while Earnest pulled on a too-tight coat and buttoned the top button. Then he joined Sonny at the mirror, where the two of them chuckled at themselves.

Sonny picked up a felt marker and scribbled on Earnest's upper lip. "Hardy has a little bitty mustache, remember?"

Earnest wiggled his upper lip. "Not bad, but this hair has to come down." He greased his hair with hair tonic and combed it straight down over his forehead.

"That looks terrific," Sonny said. "Except we need to powder our faces, like they do in the movies." He found a can of old shaving powder and smeared it on himself and Earnest.

The boys made one last check in the mirror. "Now all we need are some hats."

Earnest could find only one hat in the box. "I know," he said. "Up in the attic is a box of Halloween stuff. There's an old paper derby in there."

When the boys were fully costumed, they went to the kitchen to make some throwing pies.

"We can use these aluminum foil pans that Mom saves from those awful store-bought pies."

Sonny dug up a can of whipped cream, which he squirted into the pans. They carefully stacked the pans in a shallow cardboard box.

In a few minutes they were bouncing along towards Cherry's house with the wagon load of pies behind them. Also in the wagon were two plastic toy trumpets.

On the way they discussed their routine. "So, when I hand you the first pie as a peace offering, you grind it into my face, got it?"

And then it's World War Three," Sonny added. "I sure hope this works. What if she won't even come to the window to watch?"

"In that case, we have a lot of whipped cream to eat."

Earnest parked the wagon in the side yard, near Cherry's window. He set the box of pies on the ground, and each of the boys took a toy trumpet in hand. After one last rehearsal, Sonny stepped over to the window and rapped on it. Then he leaped back and put the trumpet to his lips.

The window shade jiggled, then a tiny hand appeared at the edge of it, and slowly the shade drew back.

Cherry looked startled at first, until she recognized the boys. But she did not smile. She did give a weak wave with her hand.

"There she is," Earnest squeaked. "Hit it!" The boys squawked on their toy trumpets, pausing now and then to hold out a hat to imaginary people passing by. As Hardy, Earnest stood very

proper, smiling at each person who passed by and shrugging his shoulders when no one donated. Sonny, as Laurel, massaged his head and sometimes bawled when no one dropped any money into his hat.

When it was plain to see they had failed as musicians, Laurel seemed to get angry with Hardy. He punched him in the eye. Hardy popped a button off Laurel's coat, and Laurel stomped on Hardy's foot.

The boys went on like this for some time: shin-kicking, coat-ripping, and eye-popping. Every now and then they glanced at the window to see if Cherry was any happier, but she wasn't.

"Okay," Sonny mumbled, "Now for the pies. Pies will do it when nothing else will."

Hardy calmed down and slowly handed Laurel a pie as a peace offering. Laurel looked at the pie, then tipped it back into Hardy's face.

The fight was on again, with pies smashing into faces and falling on feet. Pies in their hair and all over their clothes. Pies in their eyes, and pies in their ears.

At long last the boys were out of pies and energy. They tumbled to the ground and stared back at the window, but no one was there.

Sadly, Sonny gathered up the pans and loaded the wagon. The two of then wiped cream from their eyes as they turned and trudged home. Neither of them said anything. Only the *clink* and *clank* of the wagon broke the silence.

As they wheeled up the driveway, they were beginning to feel a little better. "It will just take more time," Sonny said.

"Yeah," Earnest replied. "I guess you're right. Hey, I'll race you to the house. Last one there is a ten-pound termite."

Sonny dropped the wagon handle and leaped into stride, with Earnest sprinting right behind him.

Wham! Sonny crashed through the kitchen door and screeched to a standstill. Earnest slammed into his back.

"Oops!" Sonny said in a high-pitched voice. There in front of the boys were all the ladies from church eating refreshments.

Mrs. Wheeler's eyes popped when she saw the two pie-smeared boys standing in the doorway. She gasped and clutched at her throat, choking.

"Wrong door!" Sonny sang out, and the boys whirled around and vanished like a puff of smoke.

7 • The Diamond

Earnest blinked, then opened his eyes and looked around the room. An early morning breeze ruffled his bedroom curtains, and a sparrow landed momentarily on his window sill. It vanished as quickly as it came.

Earnest started to get out of bed, but he couldn't seem to move. "What the . . ."

He tried still harder, but still he went no where. He stared down at his body. Strands of heavy twine were wrapped tightly around him, running under the bed.

"Son-ny!" he hollered. "Son-ny!"

Giggles came from the doorway and Sonny danced inside, still dressed in his underwear. He pointed at Earnest and laughed like a madman.

"You're not going to be laughing when I get out of here," Earnest threatened. He squirmed and chewed at the twine with his teeth.

"Don't get so hyper," Sonny said. "I'll cut you loose, for pity sake." He unwrapped the twine. Earnest wriggled out and dived at Sonny, pinning him to the floor. "I'm telling Dad," Earnest said. "And he is gonna beat your—"

"Go ahead and tell," Sonny dared him. "And I'll break both your arms."

Earnest dragged himself up and pulled on his slacks. "I thought we agreed, no more practical jokes. I oughta take a point off your score."

Sonny sat down on the edge of the dresser. "Awwww, I'm tired of this good deed bit. Where has it got us? We just get people upset and make ourselves good and tired."

"Relax," Earnest replied. "This is Thursday. The game's over Saturday at supper. Then you can be your old rotten self again."

"Well, I'm taking a break from it. Going over to the park."

"Okay, I'll go with you."

As the boys were leaving the house, their mother called after them. "Boys, I called Cherry. She wouldn't say much, but I think her grandmother is a little bit better. She refuses to go to the hospital."

The boys nodded and rode away toward the park.

The park was quiet as they pedaled through the shady trees. The Chariton River looked asleep, and the first yellow leaves of the year were parachuting quietly to its glassy surface.

On they pedaled, past picnickers and target shooters and joggers. They slowed down at the ball diamond, an old field not well kept and not used for organized games. They leaned their bikes against the backstop and watched the unofficial game in progress. Six bigger boys were out on the field, and the team at bat was made up of three smaller boys and two girls.

After watching a few minutes, Sonny and Earnest could see the teams were not well matched. The big guys were stomping the other team without mercy.

"What's the score?" Earnest asked a small girl who was warming up a bat.

"Thirteen to one, their favor," she said, with despair in her voice. "They don't play fair either." She stepped up to the plate and with great effort fanned her bat a couple times.

The pitcher looked at the little girl and sneered. "Hey, look what we've got here—a little rosebud, just waiting to be plucked." He bounced the ball off the ground a couple times, then spit over his shoulder. With no warning at all he fired off a fast pitch. The ball sizzled through the air. With a sickening smack it hit the little girl in her left thigh. Instantly a look of shock and pain came to her face, and she crumpled to the dust, clutching at her leg.

Her teammates rushed to her side, but she waved them away. There she lay writhing in agony, her eyes leaking large drops of pain mixed with anger.

"Hey!" Earnest yelled. "That was *deliberate*, Sonny. He beaned her on purpose. What a rotten stunt."

A fighting look formed in Sonny's eyes. He turned to Earnest, and in a firm voice said, "Earnest, I feel another good deed coming on."

The two of them dropped their bikes and tramped onto the field.

"Hey, you big jerk," Sonny hollered to the pitcher. "We're joining this team. Gonna even this up a little bit."

The pitcher looked annoyed but not sorry.

Sonny picked up the biggest bat and tapped it hard on the ground. then he rested it one-handed on his right shoulder. "Try *this* rosebud!" he yelled to the pitcher. He spit towards the pitcher's mound and fanned the bat with a loud whistling sound.

Sonny let the first two pitches go by with a look of scorn, pretending he didn't want to be bothered with them. Before the next pitch he glanced at the little girl who was sitting on the bench. He winked at her and said, "This one's for you, lady."

The pitch was high, but Sonny went out to meet it. His long arms easily stretched high into the air. There was the sound of wood hitting leather, and the ball disappeared in thin air. It was not seen again until it bounced over the centerfield fence.

The team went crazy. Sonny glanced at the little girl before walking the bases. On her face was a look of thanks mixed with revenge.

The game moved swiftly now. The team on the field began to look a little nervous, and their boasting slowed down a lot.

In half an hour the score was fifteen to thirteen, the larger boys still ahead by two. Now the smaller team was up to bat.

Two boys managed to get base hits.

Earnest stepped up to the plate and swung at three pitches in a row, but all he got was a sore arm.

Now it was the little girl's turn to bat, but she balked. She sat on the bench, shaking her head and rubbing her swollen leg.

Sonny and Earnest knelt in the dust beside her, pleading with her to take her turn. "What's the matter?" Sonny asked in a tender voice.

"I'm afraid he will hit me again," she whimpered. She rubbed her wet cheeks with her fingertips.

Sonny looked at the pitcher, then back at the little girl. "Look," he said, "I'm gonna go out there and stand right beside that goon, and if he even thinks about hitting you, I will arrange for that ball to visit the inside of his nose." The girl giggled and sniffed.

Sonny leaped up and jogged out to the pitcher's mound. He stood there with his arms crossed, spitting like someone eating watermelon.

"C'mon," Earnest pleaded with the girl. "We

really need you. You don't have to kill the ball, just get up there and wave that wood around."

The little girl looked at her leg and wiped her wet nose with her palm. Earnest could tell she was beginning to get up her courage.

"You can't run away from this," he urged her. "Running away gets to be a bad habit. Every time you run away from something it gets easier to run away the next time."

He helped her up from the bench and placed a small bat in her hand. Timidly she shuffled to the plate, and her teammates cheered her on.

Out on the mound Sonny put his nose against the pitcher's nose and said a few choice words.

At last the pitch came sailing in. It was inside, and the girl ducked away. Again Sonny eyeballed the pitcher and spit on the ground.

The next pitch was a fastball, but it was coming right for the plate. The little girl flinched, but she swung the bat and it connected. The ball grounded past the first baseman, and one runner crossed home plate. The girl tiptoed to first base. Meanwhile, the right fielder dived on the ball and fired it to third base, but the third baseman missed it. Another runner crossed the plate. Now the little girl was passing second base at a fast walk. Sonny ran along beside her shouting, "Go, girl! Go, go, go, go, go! Go all the way! All the way!"

The little girl tripped over third base. She lay there a moment, rubbing her bad leg and looking around confused.

"Get up! Get up! Go! Go!" Sonny yelled.

The girl staggered to her feet and hobbled toward home plate, but now the left fielder had the ball and he stretched back for the toss. The little girl was almost to home plate when the ball arrived through the air. The ball hit her in the middle of the back with a dull "thunk," and she crumpled on the plate in a heap.

"Oh, no!" Earnest moaned. "Not again! I can't believe it, they're trying to kill this girl."

But the ball had spent most of its force before it hit her. The little girl jumped right up, grinning ear to ear and rubbing her shoulderblade.

Sonny grabbed the girl and hoisted her to his shoulders. For several minutes the game waited while her teammates followed her around, cheering and whistling. She was laughing and crying at the same time.

The game finished out at 18 to 15 in the little team's favor.

During the ride home, Sonny winked at Earnest. "You know, Earnest, I'm beginning to get the hang of this good stuff. What's next?"

Earnest grinned back. "I don't know, but we *each* get a point for that one. Now the score is three to three."

8 • Pulling Teeth

Earnest helped his father fix breakfast Friday morning. "What's wrong with Mom?" he wanted to know. "How come she's sleeping in?"

Mr. Wheeler dropped some eggshells in the wastebasket. "Oh, you remember that meeting of the church ladies here the other night?"

Earnest nodded.

"Well, one of the ladies has a tongue like a razor blade. I guess she criticized everything your mother said and did, from the refreshments to the wallpaper. Even the clothes she was wearing."

Earnest frowned. "Hey, I'd tell the old woman to buzz off if she didn't like it here. I'd open the door and help her down the steps."

"You just don't do that, Earnest, believe me. Your mother is rather plain-spoken herself, but she would never be unkind. She would never fight back."

After breakfast, Earnest went to his room and sat at his desk to think. Then he took a sheet of typing paper and spun it into his typewriter. With two fingers he pecked out a letter.

Dear Mrs. Wheeler,

    I'm writing to tell you what a really nice time I had at your house last night. Everything was really neat. I loved the refreshments, and your house is really neat. Your taste in clothes is really good, if you ask me. Also, you were really nice to a certain lady who has a really big mouth. You should have shown her the door.

                  Sincerely,
                  A Friend

He sealed the letter, stamped it, and took it to the corner mailbox.

When he returned, Sonny was in the driveway, fixing a flat tire on his bike. Earnest sat on the grass, watching and thinking.

"You know," he said, "I feel really bad that we haven't done anything for Dad. He was the one we hurt most with our tricks."

Sonny flipped his bike upright and spun the wheel to check it. "You're right. Maybe something will show up. There, that's fixed."

"That's not the only thing around here needs fixin'," Earnest added. "We ought to fix that kitchen door that sticks. That would be a good project."

Sonny sat down on the grass beside Earnest, and he wiped the sweat from his face with his tee shirt.

"Yep, I suppose we ought to fix that door."

"And we should fill the potholes in this driveway," Earnest went on. "Dad almost broke an axle in that big one." He tossed a pebble into the hole.

"Yep," Sonny said, "we ought to do that."

"And the south side of the garage needs a coat of paint."

"Yep," Sonny said, "it sure does."

"We could wash the windows on Dad's used cars."

"Yep, they sure need it."

Earnest paused to think. "We could stack all those old tires in a neat pile and straighten up that row of old batteries."

Sonny put a fresh toothpick in his mouth. "Yep, we could."

"Or we could clean out the office."

Sonny took a deep breath and let it out slowly. "Yeah, I guess so."

Earnest glanced at the hot sun overhead. He wiped his damp brow with his arm. "We could . . . we could go swimming."

Sonny awoke from his trance. His face looked like he was staring at a plate of fresh chocolate chip cookies. "All right!" he sang out. "Now you're making sense!"

Both boys sprang to their feet and sped towards the house. In a few minutes they came bounding out again, dressed in their trunks and carrying innertubes, goggles, towels, and a plastic ball and bat. In seconds they were padding across the highway in their bare feet, then swishing through the meadow path to Long Branch Lake. Down below they could see a couple families already on the beach.

"Last one there is a fifty-pound frog," Earnest squealed.

Soon the boys tumbled on to the beach and heaved their innertubes into the blue water.

For a while they merely splashed around like puppies in a puddle. Then they played water baseball with some other kids. Last, they stretched out on their towels to soak up some sun.

While they were lying there half asleep, Earnest heard a moaning sound. At first he ignored it, thinking it was just some kids playing. The moaning came closer. He opened his eyes and sat up. Squinting, he saw a large, middle-aged man sloshing toward shore with his hand over his mouth. The man's arms were like big drumsticks and his legs were like upside-down pop bottles. His belly draped over his trunks like a big blob of putty about to drip on the ground. A thin mustache and a bald head added to his walrus look. The man wallowed up on shore, still clutching his mouth.

Earnest shook Sonny. "Look, something's wrong with that man."

The man was now standing in front of his wife, trying to explain his problem to her.

Earnest overheard the word, "teeth." Then he heard the wife say to her children, "Your father has lost his dentures in the lake."

Earnest hopped up, pulling Sonny up with him.

"Let's go, that man lost his dentures in the lake." The boys ambled over to the man.

"Where did you lose them?" Earnest asked, politely. The man pointed to a spot about twenty-five feet from shore and mumbled something through his hand.

Sonny needed to hear no more. He sprinted to the lake and dived under the waves, looking for the teeth.

Earnest asked more questions. "How far were you from that tuft of weeds sticking up? When did you notice the teeth were missing?"

At last he was satisfied. He waded in and studied the water carefully. Back and forth he waded in neat, straight rows, feeling the bottom with his toes.

Sonny popped out of the water with something in his hand. He wiped his face and looked at his catch. It was a jar lid. Back under he went.

Earnest ducked under and came up with something. He stared at it until he figured out it was just a sardine can. He walked on.

Sonny shot up. "I found 'em!" he hollered. Sure enough, in his hand were the pink and white plastic teeth. As he waded towards shore he kept waving the teeth in the air and shouting, "I found 'em,

I found 'em . . . oops!" The teeth slipped from his fingers and sank back under the waves. He looked horrified. Sonny and Earnest both dived for the teeth, their legs waving above the water like odd water flowers.

Whoosh! Sonny sprang up again with a great big grin. The teeth were in his hand. In a moment he staggered on to the beach and handed the prize to the grateful man. The man smiled a huge, toothless smile, then reached for his billfold.

"I want you to have a little something to show my appreciation," he said. He pinched a twenty-dollar bill, wadded it up, and shoved it firmly into Sonny's hand. Sonny's eyes brightened.

"Thank you, Sir, thanks very much." He played with the bill.

Earnest whispered in Sonny's ear, "If you take the money, you don't get a point for the good deed."

Sonny looked once more at the crisp bill, then at Earnest, then at the man. He handed the money back to the man. "Thanks anyway," he said in a shaky voice. "Just glad to help out."

All the way home Sonny and Earnest argued about the money.

"Just because I get paid doesn't mean it isn't a

good deed," Sonny argued. "I mean, preachers get paid for doing good things."

Earnest shook his head. "Wrong, Sonny. Preachers don't get paid for doing good. Dad says they get paid so they'll have more *time* to do good."

"Okay," Sonny grumbled, "but I've got *four* points to your three."

9 • The Big Prize

Saturday morning. Sonny sat on the edge of his bed, trying to get himself awake. He slid his feet into his slippers, but when he tried to stand up and walk he couldn't. The slippers were stuck to the floor. He teetered back and forth, trying to keep from falling on his face.

"What the . . . Earnest!"

Earnest peeked through the doorway, trying to look innocent, but his face creamed with guilt.

"That's *it*, I'm telling Dad," Sonny promised.

"I'm just getting even for when you tied me in bed, remember? You tell, and I'll tell."

Sonny peeled his slippers from the floor.

"It's just carpet tape," Earnest explained. "Hey, today is the last day of our contest. It's all over at supper."

As the boys dressed, they could hear a commotion in the kitchen. Their father was yelling something and their mother was yelling back at him.

By the time they sat down to breakfast all was quiet, but the air was tense. Mr. Wheeler sat at the table with his chin propped on his hands and a scowl on his face. His eyes were a mixture of anger and tears.

"What was all the noise about?" Sonny dared to ask. No one answered him for a long while.

Mrs. Wheeler chopped at a pan of cinnamon rolls like she was beating a snake to death. Then she said, "Your father lost an important car part, and he's blaming me for it."

"I'm not *blaming you*," Mr. Wheeler growled. He turned to the boys. "I'm working on this carburetor, see, and I have it almost back together. Then I find out I'm missing a little metal pin. One little metal pin, the size and shape of a wooden pencil tip. . . ." He fished one out of his pocket and held it up for them to see. "Like this one."

"Just buy another one," Mrs. Wheeler suggested.

"I *told* you,. the parts stores are closed today. Besides, it's a custom carb. I don't know if I can even get one."

"Where did you lose it?" Earnest asked meekly.

His father's face turned a dark pink. He stood up. "If I knew *that*, it wouldn't be lost, would it? Somewhere in the garage, that's all I know." He checked his pockets for his keys and billfold. "I'm going over to Salisbury. They have a parts store over there that's open on Saturday." He tromped towards the door, then turned around. "If I don't come back, I'm probably in Australia. Or Siberia."

"How come he's so upset over a little part?" Earnest asked his mother.

"Because. It's for a very important customer. He promised the man he would have the job done three days ago. I feel so sorry for your father. He works so hard. I don't know why these things happen to such a wonderful man."

Sonny and Earnest finished breakfast, then wandered outside. Both of them were thinking the same thoughts. Sonny went straight to the garage, and Earnest pattered along right behind him.

"First one to find the part gets *two* points," Sonny said.

"Okay, but let's get organized."

"Earnest, if you and I were the only people left on earth, you would organize us into President and Vice President."

"I'll be the President. You take the floor, and I'll take the workbenches and tool carts."

"What's the matter, Earnest, afraid you'll get your knees dirty?"

"Okay, okay, *I'll* take the floor a while, and then we can switch."

For over an hour the boys scoured the garage for the missing part. Earnest even used a magnet to skim through the dust and dirt. He stretched out flat on the floor and shined a flashlight back and forth slowly.

At long last Earnest collapsed into an old, greasy vinyl chair to rest. "That's it for me. I give up. If it's in this room, we would have found it for sure."

Sonny was still crawling around on his hands and knees, making one last check. "Ouch," he cried out. He jumped up, rubbing his knee.

"Ohhhh," I got something in my knee." He danced around on one leg and explored his knee with his hand. "There you are. Look at this, Earnest. I got this little doodad stuck in my knee." He held it out in his palm for Earnest to see, then started to toss it into the waste barrel.

"Hold it!" Earnest screamed. "That's it! That's the part we're looking for!"

Sonny squinted at the little piece of metal. "You're right. You're absolutely right. Let's face it, I've got talented knees."

Earnest cringed. "I guess that puts you in the lead, six to three."

Sonny smiled a smug smile. "Give up, Earnest. I've got you now."

When Mr. Wheeler returned from Salisbury, he looked worse than ever. Mrs. Wheeler and the boys were waiting for him in the garage office.

He shuffled into the office and collapsed into a chair. His face sagged, and his eyes were glassy with despair.

"No part?" Mrs. Wheeler asked.

Slowly he shook his head and rubbed his neck. He sighed a long, sad sigh and leaned his forehead against his hand, as if he were praying.

Earnest reached out and handed his father

a gift-wrapped package the size of a matchbox. "Here's a present for you, Dad."

His father looked up and tried to smile. "Thanks, boys, you're very thoughtful to try and cheer me up." Half-heartedly he peeled the wrapping from the small box, then pinched the lid with his thick fingers. For a moment he just stared at the carburetor part lying there on a little bed of cotton. "It's a . . . it's a . . ." Suddenly his face was transformed. All the tension and sadness melted away in one second, replaced by a look of someone who had just escaped a prison sentence.

"What the . . . where did you . . . how . . . who found this? Where?"

Sonny massaged his knee. "You wouldn't believe it if we told you."

Mr. Wheeler kissed the little part over and over again. Then he grabbed Sonny and Earnest and nearly crushed them with a hug. With a shout of "Thanks!" he disappeared into the garage.

Sonny grinned at Earnest. "Now, that's what I call a good deed."

Earnest smiled back as if to say, "Aren't we great?"

Late in the afternoon Sonny and Earnest headed down the street for Cherry's house. Earnest was holding a fresh chocolate cake his mother made for Cherry. It was covered with yellow flowers of icing, and it perfumed the air with chocolate. The clear plastic wrap that covered it was trying to blow away, and Sonny kept reaching under the wrap to snitch bits of excess icing from the plate.

"I don't think this will work," Earnest said. "Cherry is so bummed out it would take a mountain of cakes to pull her out of this."

"Yeah, I spoze you're right," Sonny replied. "But maybe the razzle dazzle of my personality will do the trick. I say whoever gets her to smile first gets *three* points."

Earnest shrugged. "Okay by me."

As the boys turned into Cherry's yard, Earnest stopped to watch the butterflies feeding on Cherry's flower garden. He clutched the cake in his left hand and slowly reached for a yellow butterfly with his right hand. The butterfly fluttered away. Earnest followed it. Again he reached for it, and again it moved, this time to the center of the garden. Earnest stood on tiptoe and stretched to reach the yellow wings that slowly opened and closed on a red zinnia.

"Uh-oh," he said. He lost his footing and

crashed into the bed of flowers with a swooshing sound. He clung tightly to the cake. Too tightly. The cake crushed against his chest and neck, oozing chocolate icing all over his face and shoulder.

"Ohhhhh," he moaned. "I think I'm gonna spit."

Suddenly he heard giggles. He looked up. There on the porch stood Cherry, giggling like someone was tickling her. She pointed at Earnest with one hand and adjusted the strap of her white dress with the other.

"Cherry! You're laughing!" Sonny shouted. "You're laughing!"

She skipped down the steps and helped Sonny pull Earnest out of the flower bed.

"Hey, I'm sorry about your flowers," Earnest said. "I guess we messed up everything for you."

"Yeah," Sonny added. "We were trying to cheer you up, but everything seemed to go wrong."

"You guys are so silly," Cherry sang out. "You haven't done *anything* wrong. You're the best friends I've got." In the bright sun her face blushed like a ripe peach, and her hair shone like polished brass.

"But those chocolate truffles were ruined by the hot sun."

"That wasn't your fault. Besides, I ate 'em anyhow. I can eat chocolate any way you want to serve it."

"And that Laurel and Hardy thing," Sonny interrupted. "Boy, was that a dumb idea."

"Well, *I* didn't think it was dumb," Cherry said sweetly. "I *loved* it."

"But you didn't laugh. And when we were all done you were gone."

Cherry giggled again. "I was on the *floor*, silly! When you started the pie fight, I got to laughing so hard I fell down. Plop! Right on the floor." She acted it out with her little hands.

"How's your grandma?" Earnest asked.

"She's all well, now, the doctor says." Cherry hung her head and rubbed the toes of her sandals together. "I got real scared when Grandma got sick. I don't have anybody to take care of me if something happens to her." She blinked, then the smile returned to her face.

"Thanks, you guys," she said. "I really mean it."

The boys nodded. "Well, we've got to go," Sonny said. "But am I ever glad to see you smiling again."

On the way home Earnest said, "I guess the score is even, six to six. I get three points for making Cherry laugh." He glanced at his watch. "We've got time for one more good thing if you want to break the tie."

Sonny looked puzzled. "You know what? We didn't decide on a prize for this contest."

Earnest scratched his head. "You're right! We must be slipping. I didn't even write up a contract."

The boys walked along in silence for a few minutes. Then Earnest cleared his throat to speak. "Sonny . . . I don't feel right about getting points for doing good stuff."

"How come?"

"I dunno. It just seems like we already won a prize, just seeing some neat things happen."

Sonny nodded. "I'll never forget that little girl at the baseball diamond. What a trooper!"

"And the look on Mom's face when she saw how clean the house was?"

"And Dad, don't forget him. You'd think we gave him a check for a million dollars when we handed him that car part."

Sonny chuckled to himself. "Remember that patrolman at the post office? Boy, was he disappointed. He was sure he had caught two criminals in the act."

Earnest held out his hand. "What say we call it a draw?"

Sonny looked at Earnest's hand and hesitated for a long time. Then he grasped the hand and squeezed it firmly. "Tie game," he said. "The best *men* won."

10 • Five Special Words

On their way to church Sunday morning, the Wheelers stopped to pick up Cherry. She sat in back between the boys. She wore a bright red dress and a small matching hat. Earnest was dressed in his three-piece suit and wore rings on his fingers. Sonny looked uncomfortable in his dress slacks and shirt.

"Boys, how did your little project turn out?" Mrs. Wheeler asked, trying to break the silence.

"We tied," Sonny mumbled. He was busy watching out the window.

"It wasn't as easy as I thought," Earnest added. "Sometimes doing good things gets a little tricky."

"Speaking of good things," Mrs. Wheeler said, "I got one of the nicest letters yesterday from one of the ladies at church. She didn't sign it, but she said the sweetest things. Made me feel so good after all that criticism I got the other night."

Earnest looked at his toes and blushed. When he looked back up, his mother was smiling at him. Then she winked.

Earnest grinned sheepishly, realizing he had not fooled his mother with the unsigned letter. He winked back.

Mr. Wheeler flipped on the turn signal and glanced back at the boys. "I'm sure glad you two found that carb part, or I might be in the hospital right now." He shook his head, chuckling to himself.

The church was crowded when they arrived, but they managed to find a seat near the front.

"How come so many people are here today?" Sonny asked his father in a low voice.

"Because we have a new preacher, remember? Everybody probably wants to see what he's like."

"I like the old preacher better," Earnest said.

"How do you know if you haven't even met the new one?" his mother asked.

The preacher walked out on to the platform. He was young and muscular-looking and he seemed to know what he was doing. Earnest noticed how well he was dressed.

"He drives a convertible," Mr. Wheeler whispered to Sonny. "A *red* convertible."

Sonny arched his eyebrows and snickered.

"And he likes to fish and hunt and swim," Mr. Wheeler added.

At last it was time for the sermon. Sonny and Earnest shifted in their seats, preparing for a long sit.

"My sermon today is about five words," the preacher began. "Five special words. Five words that can change the world." He opened his Bible.

Sonny blinked at Earnest.

The preacher went on. "If you follow the example of these five words they will change your life and the lives of your family and friends. They will change the people of your community and your world."

Earnest looked at Sonny as if to say, "Wonder what five words can do that?"

The preacher continued. "These five words explain why thousands of people followed Jesus all around Palestine. And if you do these five words, you too will be popular with people."

Sonny and Earnest sat up straighter and fixed their eyes on the preacher.

"Anybody can do these five words," the preacher explained. "Anybody, anywhere. It doesn't require a lot of money, but it will make a big difference in lives."

Sonny punched his father with his elbow. "When's he gonna tell us the five words?"

His father just shrugged his shoulders.

The preacher thumbed through his Bible. "If you follow these five words," he said, "you will never be bored. Your life will be full of interesting experiences and you will feel a happiness you could know in no other way. You will feel important and needed."

Cherry smiled at Sonny and Earnest as if to say, "*You* make me feel important." The boys blushed.

"The five words I'm thinking of are found in the book of Acts, in the tenth chapter." The preacher held his Bible close to his face, so he could see the fine print in the dimly-lighted auditorium.

Sonny grabbed a Bible from the pew rack, and Earnest pulled a pen and a card from his pocket.

"Here are the five words that can change the world. Five words about the life of Jesus. They are found in the thirty-eighth verse of the tenth chapter of Acts. I will read them slowly for you."

Sonny quickly found the tenth chapter and began skimming the verses with his finger. Earnest poised his pen to write.

The minister cleared his throat. "And here are the five words. I quote: '*He . . . went . . . about . . . doing . . . good.*'" For each word he held up another finger as he read them. The minister repeated the five words, then closed his Bible.

Sonny looked at Earnest, who was looking back at him. "Hey!" he whispered. "He's talking about *us!* That's what we just did."

"Yeah," Earnest muttered. "That's us all right. You know, I think I'm gonna like this preacher after all."

Wheeler's Adventures

Wheeler's Deal

Sonny and Earnest challenge each other to see who can be the first to earn $100.

Wheeler's Big Catch

During a time the boys are not getting along, they challenge each other to a fishing contest.

Wheeler's Ghost Town

A local newspaper sponsors a news writing contest, with a TV appearance for the winner.

Wheeler's Good Time

Forbidden from playing any more practical jokes, the boys see how many good deeds they can do in one week.